The Lies We Know

LIANA BROOKS

OTHER WORKS

ALL I WANT FOR CHRISTMAS

All I Want For Christmas Is A Reaper
All I Want For Christmas Is A Werewolf

FLEET OF MALIK

Bodies In Motion
Change of Momentum

HEROES AND VILLAINS

Even Villains Fall In Love
Even Villains Go To The Movies
Even Villains Have Interns
Even Villains Play The Hero (omnibus)
The Polar Terror

TIME AND SHADOWS
The Day Before
Convergence Point
Decoherence

SHORTER WORKS

Fey Lights
Prime Sensations
Darkness and Good

Find other works by the author at
www.lianabrooks.com

The Lies We Know

INKLET #56

LIANA BROOKS

www.inkprintpress.com

Print ISBN: 978-1-925825-58-9
eBook ISBN: 9781393049081

www.inkprintpress.com

National Library of Australia Cataloguing-in-Publication Data
Brooks, Liana 1982 –
The Lies We Know
46 p.
ISBN: 978-1-925825-58-9
Inkprint Press, Canberra, Australia
1. Fiction—Science Fiction—Space Opera 2. Fiction—Science Fiction—Action & Adventure 3. Fiction—Short Stories

First Print Edition: April 2021
Cover design © Inkprint Press
Interior art © Amy Laurens

THE LIES WE KNOW

"REMEMBER, YOU'RE ALL GOING TO DIE eventually. Might as well make it worthwhile."

As pep talks went, the commander's was down with the likes of 'Let's all get killed!', but he seemed convinced he had a point. The problem was, he didn't. I knew he was wrong. My whole life had proved him wrong.

Most people died eventually. But life is all about probability and statistics. There are no absolutes. Even death, a penultimate absolute that claims 99.999999% of the population, isn't truly an absolute. There's always that .000001%. Me.

Everyone clamped their helmets tight shut against the vacuum of space. We were going into battle against overwhelming odds and we needed to make them underwhelming odds before the Kanfir ships reached the jump for the Euon Ri system.

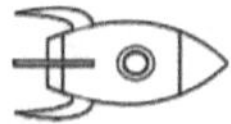

Thirty-seven hours later, I was the only survivor, and the captured Kanfir flag ship was arguing with me.

"I cannot obey that order."

"Kendla sentient ship! I don't care what you think you can or cannot do, change course before we hit the sun!"

"I cannot obey that order. A senior line officer must enter the course change into the log book."

I banged my head on the soft, somewhat gummy edge of the ship's interface. "Is there a senior line officer left alive?"

"No."

Didn't think so. The Kanfir hadn't anticipated us swarming their ships with soldiers in aerial jets meant for orbital station work. The barges had closed, we'd shot off across the vacuum, and watched as the empty barges burn behind us. It was a suicide mission. Sort of. Not for me, per se, but for everyone else. "Are there any junior officers left alive?"

I didn't want to go into the sun, but this ship was the last one left with working navigation controls.

Sort of. The Kanfir captain had burned the override interface before we took their control room, but the ship itself was alive. I didn't know enough about the Kanfir to know if the ship was a species they'd caught and enslaved, or if they'd created these behemoths in some lab, but whatever the creature's history, it was bent on driving me to insanity.

"I can find no junior officers," the ship reported after a moment, sounding ever-so-slightly distressed.

"Go down the chain of command and let me know when you find someone who can be promoted to senior line officer in the event of catastrophic loss of life."

"I have three thousand nine hundred and seventeen individuals who fit those parameters."

"Is one of them alive?"

The ship was silent for a moment. "Yes."

I looked up at the amber-brown hull in surprise. "On this ship? Alive?"

"Yes."

"Where?" I checked the charge on my gun. Still above thirty percent. Good enough for government work.

"Second Sergeant Bradford Rios is in temporary stasis in medical hold twenty-nine B," the ship said.

"Is that the medical ward with a hole gaping into the vacuum of space?"

"Yes." There was a cricket chirp and the ship added, "Should I focus repair energies on that ship section?"

Ten days until we hit the critical point of maneuvers and were too close to the sun to escape.

"Sure. Repair away. Let me know when I can go rescue the new commanding officer."

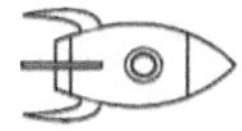

Eight days later, I'd reached a wary understanding with the ship. It gave me correct information promptly, and I didn't stab it with an electroblade.

Electroblades are antique—kind of like me. Illegal just about everywhere

I've been, but they're so rare that no one bothers to ask if you're carrying one. No sentient alive likes their flesh sliced while electricity floods their system. It's horribly painful, leaves scars that take decades to heal, and memories that never fade. Ask me how I know.

"Moira?" the ship said as I heaved another oversized Kanfir body into the airlock I was using as a dumping ground. Whatever they'd been feeding these boys, it was heavy in protein. Felin heavy bodies, all muscle and nice to look at—but pretty didn't stop bullets and it didn't make my disposal job any easier.

I slammed my fist against the lock plate. "Yes?"

"Medical hold twenty-nine B is secured and airtight. Would you like me to begin recovery of Second Sergeant Bradford Rios?"

"Yes please."

There was the cricket-like chirp I'd come to dread; the ship had found something that was going to cause an argument. "Second Sergeant Bradford Rios is under stasis lock for another ninety-two years, by the ship's working calendar."

I raised an eyebrow. "What for?"

"Treason, disobedience to a direct order, questioning a superior officer, blasphemy, violence, obstruction of justice, drunk or disorderly conduct, seventeen weapons infractions involving possession of a weapon or device of non-regulation origin, four weapons infractions involving discharge of a deadly weapon in a restricted area, fourteen weapons infractions involving failure to pass mandatory weapons inspections, and failure to complete a five kilometer run in under twenty minutes standard."

"Sounds like a real gem," I said. "Wake our boy up and let him know that he has been promoted to senior captain of the fleet."

"Admiral," the ship corrected. "But I do not believe the Second Sergeant can obtain the rank of Admiral with these charges against him. It's unprecedented."

"Did you find another beating heart on this tugboat?"

"Only you." The ship might have been a fleshy AI, but it made 'you' sound like the foulest curse word in the galaxy.

"Well then, it's me or your Boy Wonder for fleet admiral. Who would you rather answer to?"

"Beginning defrost sequence for Fleet Admiral Bradford Rios," the ship said quickly. "Estimated conscious alertness in thirty-eight minutes."

"Plenty of time."

I tidied up, dumped the bodies out the airlock, sorted hand weapons and other gewgaws I'd stripped off the dead, and wandered down to the newly restored medical bay.

I had to get myself one of these ships.

Self-repairing battleship? Be still my cold heart!

No matter how well-built a ship was, it eventually fell apart. Time destroyed things.

Most things.

I'd watched cultures rise and fall. Empires that came and went in the blink of an eye. Sometimes *really* in the blink of an eye. Most revolutions don't last more than a year or two, something historians forget because a year of anarchy always feels like an eternity.

The ship's medical hold was a barracks-style room with several dozen medical cots separated by membranous tissue the same amber-gold as the rest of the ship's interior.

Before alpha battalion had punched a hole in the side, there'd probably been blankets, and hand-held medical scanners, and the rest of the usual doctor paraphernalia. Now there was a Kanfir man in a clean engineering sergeant's uniform lying on a silver table, lips tinged blue.

"He is alive still, right? You didn't wake him up wrong?"

"The stasis chamber was below optimal temperature when the skitters retrieved the fleet admiral," the ship replied, "but he is within recovery range."

"Not brain dead?"

"There is a forty percent chance of brain damage with this procedure."

Not that the ship or I were likely to notice unless the damage left him drooling. Rios hadn't sounded like he was firing all pistons up top to begin with.

"Do you have a blanket or anything? He looks cold."

A cricket chirp. "Internal sensors cannot find anything similar to a blanket onboard. The stores room was completely destroyed, as were the barracks."

A lucky hit.

We'd caught the Kanfir ground forces sleeping in their bunks while the zoomies swatted at space gnats. Fly boys couldn't fight hand-to-hand like the infantry, not without a few drinks on them, and the loss of the entire infantry force of Kanfir in a single hit was more demoralizing to them than I'd expected.

"Fleet Admiral Rios is waking," the ship reported.

I turned to my new comrade at arms.

Time to play nice.

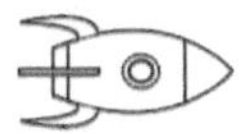

Ford blinked his eyes at the harsh light. There was a little knick in the lamp cover. Either he'd been dragged out of stasis sleep on the Subtle Queen or someone had put up a fight going down. Icy nightmares clung in his mind. Shadows tugged at him even now—the last of the stasis drugs burning out of his body, he hoped. Stasis was hell.

"Wakey wakey, Admiral," a sardonic female voice said.

He turned, expecting to see one of her majesty's own medtechs, and instead saw a girl no more than twenty, wearing blood-red space armor and flipping a knife with a blade made of lightning. Fleet had clearly changed in the ninety-five years he'd spent tied in the shadows.

She winked at him. "How you feeling?"

Ford sat up slowly. The shadows tried to drag him down, but he made it upright. "Nauseous."

"I hear that happens after stasis."

He looked around the empty medical hold. "Doctor?"

The stranger shook her head. "Long story. Let's focus instead on the positive things, okay? Like your promotion."

Straight to her majesty's own slave mine. Ford grunted and watched the woman sheath her knife.

"You are the new fleet admiral." Her smile was cheerful and youthful, wholly at odds with her body language.

He smiled mirthlessly. "I wouldn't be promoted to anything in fleet unless everyone died, and even then it would be a long shot."

She nodded. "Funny story that. I'll tell you as we walk."

Ford tried to stand. The floor felt alien under his socks. "I need boots."

"What size?"

"Nine and three-quarters."

"Do you mind if they have blood on them?" She looked perfectly serious.

"Why not get them from ship stores?"

She wrinkled her nose. "There's a tiny problem with the ship stores."

"Queenie?" Ford said, calling for the ship.

"Fleet Admiral Rios?" the Subtle Queen replied evenly in Her Majesty's voice.

He shook his head. Unbelievable. "Queenie, may your humble penitent retrieve new boots and gear from the ship's stores?"

"Request denied," the Queen said.

"The ship doesn't have stores," the girl added. "There's now a gaping hole where the blankets used to be."

"And where are the Queen's Men?" Ford asked.

"Dead." The girl shrugged.

The cold shock rolled over him in a soft wave. It wasn't wholly unexpected. Only total devastation would bring the fleet to need him as a soldier of any kind. "What happened?"

Famine? Attack? Another internal coup between rival princesses?

"Me, mostly." The girl smiled. "You can call me Moira."

He stared at her childlike face. "You?"

"Like I said, long story. Now, let's walk over to the control room, and you can tell the ship to change course so we don't run into the sun. Then we'll have a nice long talk about astrochartography, political realities, and the chances of you living to see another meal. M'kay?"

Possibilities and theories freewheeled through his mind until Ford caught hold of one reality. "We're diving into the sun?"

"Yes, and we have less than forty-eight hours to correct course before we're stuck with it. If you can't get the ship to obey, I'm going to need some time to find another way to reprogram this beast."

Ford stopped short. "You can't re-program a celestial queen! She responds only to the voice of Her Majesty or the Queen's Men who fight for her life and honor!"

Moira looked unmoved. "I know where the brain center is. Talk the ship into changing course, or your queen gets a lobotomy."

Ford stared at her. "Are all women like you?"

"All the women you need to worry about."

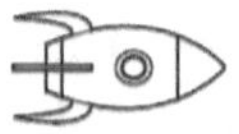

The former sergeant wasn't happy with his sudden change of rank. His body language shifted as we walked down the deserted halls, still splashed with dried blood. In the medical hold he'd been depressed but mostly relaxed, reacting slowly. The further we walked, the tenser he became. Muscles bunched up in his shoulders. His fists curled. His stride became a defiant march past the field of battle now a week old.

"They're all dead?"

"It was the Kanfir or the Euonians." I shrugged. "That's the thing about wars. People die."

He shook his head. "It wasn't war. Her Majesty's children required new suns to graze near. The fleet was called to search the star paths for the coming swarm."

"Swarm? Like… insect swarm?"

He frowned. "Know you nothing of the Kanfir?"

"Hyper-violent male race with enslaved females kept locked on their home planet. You guys come in, kill everyone, and then abandon the systems you've destroyed."

He stopped walking and stared.

I rolled my eyes. "I've seen it done in Gretchuia and Rison. Don't deny it. I saw the senate house of Dreul when you were done in the Gretchuia system. There was nothing left. Even the stones were dust."

"Because Her Majesty ordered the place prepared for her brood!" he protested. "Her Majesty called. We cannot disobey her will."

"You need a new government," I said.

He shook his head violently this time. "No. No. You mistake me. Us. Her Majesty owns us. We are the Queen's Men. We cannot disobey. Not 'We don't think about disobeying', or 'We don't want to disobey', or 'We all agree with Her Majesty'. We *cannot* go against her. She is the Life Giver and the Life Taker. There is no way but hers. When she wishes to lay a clutch, we obey and clear land, and now her daughters seek to swarm, to take suns of their own. We obey or we die."

"Or you obey and still die." I smiled. "Looks like a lose-lose situation all around." I led him to the control room. "Does this whole queen business mean I can't take over the ship at all, ever?"

"The ship is the Subtle Queen. It is a piece of Her Majesty, and extension of her will and dominion."

"I'm not actually hearing a no here."

The sergeant stalked over to the control console and stared. "I was never trained for this."

"No worries. I know what I'm do-ing." I showed him how to call up the screen and set various coordinates.

"I should take us home," he said.

I shook my head. "Bad idea. At home you still have a prison sentence to live out. Let's go somewhere fun. Escinia is nice this time of year. Or the Sertian colonies. I hear they're making great progress with the swamp plagues. We can go, find new jobs, loiter on a beach somewhere, make new friends... It'll be great!"

He stared at her. "These are not places I have ever heard of."

"Again, no worries. When I was growing up I'd never heard of them either."

I gave him the coordinates to Sertian space. They were a disorganized group with multiple governments on each of their three settled planets and they promised to have an interesting future. It was somewhere a person could get lost in the tides of humanity.

The sergeant sat reluctantly, then turned. "Where were you born? Far from here? On Dreul perhaps?"

"I was born in San Francisco on this cute little planet called Earth."

He frowned. "That is an Elder Planet, one long forgotten, the Star Paths to it closed."

I shrugged. "I didn't say I was born recently. I mean, when I was a kid the big excitement was that man had walked on the moon. Interstellar travel was a fiction then." I snorted in amusement. "I thought driving eight hours to see my grandma on holidays was a big adventure because we crossed a desert."

"But... you're a child!" He held his hand near my head. "You're not grown yet."

I smiled. "I'm short. I'm not a kid."

"You are still young."

"Younger than the universe maybe, but not as young as I look." I sat down in the first officer's chair. "I visited Dreul when they were building the senate house. That was nearly three hundred years ago. I remember the system was found by a probe from

Xalian. It was all over the news for months. New world found! Habitable planet!" I waved my hands, feigning enthusiasm. "Everyone was so excited and then there were arguments over whether the Xalian river gods approved of Dreul. Once they found the gold river it was fine, of course. Obviously a heaven planet. People rioted for a chance to go. The murder rate sextupled over-night. Crazy times."

Rios sat beside me in the captain's chair. "You learned all this as a child?"

"I lived all that as an adult. An old woman. Very old." I shrugged.

"You don't look old."

"Aging is the decay of telomeres. Your body stops replicating the cells correctly. Mutations take over. You fall apart. You die. I don't. I have no cellular mutations."

"That's very strange."

"Truly freakish," I agreed.

"Impossible," the ship chimed in. "There is no similar anomaly on record."

I looked at the amber ceiling. "How many times was I shot during the initial assault on this vessel?"

"Nineteen direct hits recorded," the ship said petulantly.

"Do we need to have another talk about behaving?" I flipped open my electroknife.

There was a cricket chirp from the ship. "No."

"Didn't think so."

I smiled for the Kanfir's benefit. "Don't worry about it. I'm a freak. I was born this way. I'd say I'll die this way, but, well, that'd be a lie."

"It seems many things in life are lies," he murmured.

For a moment I wondered if I'd have to use the electroblade on him to get him to cooperate, but abruptly he placed both hands on the console.

He smiled at me, a toothy, hungry thing that hardened his eyes. "And you'll show me the universe," he said.

My own smile stretched wider in response. "I'll show you the universe."

"Then I'd better turn us around."

As he reset the course, I sighed and felt the tension in my shoulders release. I had all of eternity left at my disposal; might as well make it worthwhile.

THE MAKING OF
THE LIES WE KNOW

The universal truths are death and taxes, but what if they weren't?

Prior to industrialization, living with immortality was easy enough: you just changed villages every twenty years or so. Maybe bequeathed your inheritance to a young relative before 'dying' while traveling abroad.

In the age of computers, cameras, and DNA testing, it seems like immortality would be a bit of a burden.

So, naturally, I had to write an immortal character on a spaceship.

Read more by Liana Brooks!

PRIME SENSATIONS

"Unidentified vessel, we are Waste Hauler 133 out of Darrian 6. We carry no trade or crew," the ship's AI droned in a bored monotone.

Lana dropped into the waste hauler's modified control booth and took over. "Unidentified vessel, be advised. I steer like a drunken moose, alter your course." The reverb over the frequently patched comm lines made her sound like an old man with a lifelong bitter-root habit.

Sweat dripped down her nose. The waste hauler had a hull thirty years older than she was, and an environmental system older than that. It had survived two major system wars by being too worthless to target. And Lana was well aware that, as a debtor working off her ransom to the Iloni nation, she was slightly less valuable than the ship.

The comm crackled and she thought she heard the word "boarding."

"Unidentified vessel," she replied, "I am deaf and blind. I give you no authorization to come near this vessel. If you keep to your projected course I will have no choice but to heartlessly smash your hull because of physics."

The other ship tried to respond.

Lana grimaced and tried to compensate for the ancient communications array. "Mass times acceleration, unidentified vessel. I can't slow down in time."

"Waste Hauler 133, this is the *Marsail* out of Port Tael, flying the flag of the Exaner Confederation. Prepare to be boarded."

Black holes and dark nights! Port Tael was a pirate station, taken by the outer rim unification during the Apex

War, and currently under stars only knew which warlord.

She leaned against the rough metal of the control booth. They probably wanted to pick over the hauler for parts. Stars knew there was enough wreckage welded in to rebuild a fleet. She should probably get dressed.

Lana sniffed her armpit. Maybe a shower was in order. And clothes. And snacks. The *Marsail* wouldn't cross paths with her hauler for a few more hours, and it was the most exciting thing to happen since she'd been taken as a prisoner of war three years ago.

A shower and change of clothes later, Lana watched as the *Marsail* managed to land on the bulky waste hauler with a finesse Lana would have envied a few years ago, back when she'd thought her rift rat piloting skills would be enough to win the attention she craved.

It never had.

She tossed a boiled nut into her mouth and watched the pirate crew's slow progress through the hull. If there'd been someone to bet against, she would have wagered they'd go for the hard metals compartment, maybe grab some radiated shielding or a new engine converter.

Her second bet was the food waste department, where they might try panning for seeds. Not that it would do them any good—the Iloni poisoned the food waste to ensure the vegetation of Darrian 6 wasn't sold on the black market—but they were welcome to try.

The enemy ship latched on like a leech and sliced through her hull. The crew moved methodically toward the control deck.

If she'd had a weapon, she would have gone out to meet them. The only gear worth having was the bits she'd salvaged. Not enough to build a shuttle, not yet, but in another year or three she'd have a means of escape. If they took that...

Lana eyed the console and considered the maneuvers she'd need to shake the smaller ship off. Scrapping them against the mine corridor that kept her from diverting off course sounded promising.

She was running over the possible course corrections needed when someone banged on the door of the control booth.

"Pilot?" The person hammered on the door again. "Waste Hauler Pilot, open this door."

She raised an eyebrow and grabbed another boiled nut. Telling the intruder she'd survived far worse than they could dish out was a waste of oxygen. Right now, she was breathing. If that changed in the next few minutes, no one was going to care, least of all her.

"Open this door or we will open it for you."

"Be my guest."

"Stand back."

She looked around at the cramped booth, a cylinder of buttons, viewing screens, and control panels. Given enough time and the right tools, she could rip out the main radar and stuff herself into the box, but that would take at least an hour.

The door in front of her radiated heat.

Lana lifted the chair that had long ago rusted loose just in time to prevent hot metal shrapnel from hitting her face. "Hi." She set the chair down so she could look into the black faceplate of her attacker. With a smile, she slapped the panic button that sent the waste hauler into a death spiral, alarm beacons screaming. "Iloni forces will be here within the hour. Do you want to shoot me now, or later?" The increased gravity of the spiral pulled at her. For a moment it looked like her attacker planned on retreating. She winked at the black face mask. "Pretty girl got your tongue?"

The invader pushed past her, boots scrapping along the floor, and fumbled to hit the bypass code with large hands. "You think I don't know that trick?"

"You think I care what you know?"

The faceplate cleared as he turned to her. And Lana found herself staring into the shocked eyes of Kaleb Hath—the man who'd left her for dead.

Lana's nails bit into her palms as her fists clenched.

"Commander Hath," she said, "if I'd known it was you, I would have vented my oxygen an hour ago."

Keep reading! Head to:
www.inkprintpress.com/
lianabrooks/primesensations/
to buy your copy now!

ABOUT THE AUTHOR

Liana Brooks hasn't died yet, but she's fairly certain she isn't immortal. With the limited lifespan she's been given Liana enjoys writing science fiction in every form, from sprawling space operas romances (the *Fleet of Malik* series) to the antics of a super-powered family (the *Heroes and Villains* series).

Liana also maintains a soft spot for paranormal romances. She writes the popular *All I Want For Christmas* novellas, including *All I Want For Christmas Is A Werewolf* and *All I Want For Christmas Is A Reaper*.

You can learn more about her and her books at www.LianaBrooks.com

INKLETS

Collect them all! Released on the 1st and 15th of each month.

INKLET #055
Allure
AMY LAURENS

The LIES We KNOW
LIANA BROOKS

INKLET #057
AFTERMATH & Fool Me Once
AMY LAURENS

INKLET #058
Purity
An Age Of Unicorns Story
AMY LAURENS

INKLET #059
Saved
AMY LAURENS

INKLET #060
A Kiss is the Secret
AMY LAURENS

INKLET #061
A Changing Tales Story
Fire Bright
AMY LAURENS

INKLET #062
Hades AND Persephone
LIANA BROOKS

INKLET #063
Just So Long As You're Happy
AMY LAURENS

INKLET #064
Theft Of A Lifetime
LIANA BROOKS

INKLET #065
Shoe
AMY LAURENS

INKLET #066
Published AUTHOR
LIANA BROOKS

DOUBLE ISSUE
INKLET #067
THE REMARKABLE INSIGHT OF JELLYBEANS & Understanding
AMY LAURENS

INKLET #068
Desperate Measures
AMY LAURENS

INKLET #069
Rock-a-bye
LIANA BROOKS

INKLET #070
the Other Carly
AMY LAURENS

INKLET #071
Bs By Bioluminescent light
AMY LAURENS

INKLET #072
Even Villains Grant Wishes
A Heroes & Villains Story
LIANA BROOKS